AERIALS
AND ENVY

BY JAKE MADDOX

text by
Margaret Gurevich

STONE ARCH BOOKS
a capstone imprint

Jake Maddox JV Girls books are published by
Stone Arch Books
a Capstone imprint
1710 Roe Crest Drive
North Mankato, Minnesota 56003

www.mycapstone.com

Copyright © 2018 Stone Arch Books

Cataloging-in-Publication Data is available on the Library of Congress website.
ISBN: 978-1-4965-5914-2 (library binding)
ISBN: 978-1-4965-5916-6 (paperback)
ISBN: 978-1-4965-5918-0 (eBook PDF)

Summary: Gymnast Tamaya Jackson doesn't feel like she gets the attention she wants, despite being the team captain. But a local news station is about to change all that with a story about the gymnastics team, complete with an interview with Tamaya. Will the recognition be more than Tamaya bargained for?

Designer: Lori Bye

Image Credits:
Shutterstock: cluckva, back cover, 90-95, (background), Eky Studio, chapter openers (background), Polina Maltseva, back cover, chapter openers, (silhouette), roibu, cover

Printed and bound in Canada.
010807S18

TABLE OF CONTENTS

CHAPTER 1

A BAD DAY

Tamaya Jackson leaned into a straddle stretch. She rested her elbows on the worn, green mat in front of her. Her shoulder-length, curly hair was pulled back with a blue velvet scrunchy that matched her leotard.

She had three tests today and a project to work on when she got home. But for now, she was going to focus on gymnastics. No matter how hard her day had been, all her worries disappeared whenever she entered the gym.

If they didn't, she was good at forcing them out of her head. She needed to concentrate on what mattered most: gymnastics.

"Yo, Jackson!" yelled her teammate Natalia. She had just completed a routine on the vault across the room. Wisps of her dark hair had fallen out of her ponytail. "Mrs. Kraft gave a killer test today, huh?"

Tamaya closed her eyes and rolled onto her stomach. She reached behind her, grabbed her ankles, and pulled them to her head. "No school talk in the sacred room, Nat!" she called back.

"The captain has spoken," giggled Fatima. She raised herself on the uneven bars and did a flip.

Tamaya smiled. Hearing "captain" always made her happy. She worked hard to get that title. When seventh grade ended last year, Coach Shelly pulled her aside and complimented her on all her hard work. "Don't think I haven't noticed your drive," she'd said. "You deserve to be our captain."

That meant a lot to Tamaya. She loved gymnastics. She never thought twice about making an effort. But being noticed for all that hard work was also important to her.

Tamaya finished stretching. She hit play on her phone to practice her floor routine. Her favorite song, "In the Moment," came on. She swayed her hips to the beat. She had been practicing this routine for months. The regional competition at Orton High was only two weeks away. It was important the routine be perfect. However, she still had trouble with two tumbling passes.

As the music sped up, Tamaya took a deep breath. She swung her arms and powered her legs to give herself the momentum she needed to hurl herself into the air. Her toes bounced off the mat. She sailed high above the floor. Her goal was to do two flips in the air and briefly tap the mat with her toes. Then she'd launch into a back-handspring routine. The sequence would end with two aerials.

Tamaya somersaulted into the air twice. *Bam!* She landed on the mat as planned. *Yes!*

She quickly took a breath and raised her arms behind her. Her feet flew over her head as her back arched into the handspring. Tamaya's hands tapped the mat as her body moved itself into handstand position. Then her feet were back on the floor.

Rinse and repeat two more times, she told herself.

Tamaya knew the tumbling, back handspring, and aerial combination would set her apart from the gymnasts in the other schools. Kennedy Middle School had ranked first in the state for middle schools and junior highs the past three years. Tamaya didn't want to end that streak.

She moved to the music like lightning. One back handspring followed the other. *Success!* She raised her arms in the air, took a quick breath, and readied herself for the aerial, a no-handed cartwheel.

Tamaya had done these before, but she always tired out when she had to perform them as part of her floor routine. Especially two in a row.

Here I go, she thought. Tamaya raised her left leg forward while hopping slightly on her right leg. Then she planted her left leg on the mat and lowered her arms to her waist. She kicked off with her back leg to force herself into the air.

Her feet were in cartwheel position, but something was wrong. She twisted her torso too much. Tamaya felt herself falling. She quickly put her hands down to protect her head.

Grrr! She banged her fist on the mat.

She turned off her music and watched Coach Shelly work with Fatima on the uneven bars. Fatima rocked the bars. When Tamaya wanted a break from her own head, she watched Fatima. She was awed by the height of Fatima's giant, a move that had her rotating 360 degrees around the bar while fully extended.

Normally Tamaya enjoyed Fatima's complicated moves. Today was different. The more she watched Coach Shelly help Fatima work out the kinks of her dismount, the more Tamaya grew frustrated.

"Coach Shelly," said Tamaya, walking up to the bars, "I'm having trouble with my aerials. Can you please help?"

Coach Shelly held up her pointer finger in response. That meant Tamaya would have to wait. Coach instructed Fatima as she finished her dismount. The gymnast's feet stuck the landing perfectly.

"Great job, Fatima!" Coach Shelly called. "I see you've been practicing."

Tamaya bristled. She'd been practicing too.

"Tamaya, you and I worked on the aerials yesterday. I need to help Fatima today." Coach Shelly smiled. "Keep practicing. We'll see where you are with them tomorrow."

What Coach Shelly said was true. She had helped Tamaya yesterday, but she still needed help today. Fatima seemed to know what she was doing. And Fatima wasn't captain.

Tamaya walked back to her mat and watched the other girls doing their floor, beam, and vault routines. They were all sticking their landings. Every single one.

Tamaya felt hot tears burn behind her eyes. She quickly swiped at them with the back of her hand. She wasn't even sure why she was this upset. Was it because she was scared she was going to fail? Was it because she felt she wasn't getting the help she needed?

"Keep it up, Fatima!" she heard Coach Shelly say.

Tamaya's shoulders slumped as she tried her routine one more time. This time, she only managed one flip.

"What's going on?" asked Coach Shelly.

Tamaya jumped. She hadn't realized her coach was there.

Tamaya shrugged. "I'm having a bad day."

Coach Shelly put her hand on Tamaya's shoulder. "It happens. Tomorrow will be better."

Tamaya nodded. Coach Shelly walked away to work with Ivelisse on the vault.

Tamaya felt the tears again. This time she knew why. She wanted Coach Shelly to say, "That's a tough routine, Tamaya, but you can do it." Or, "I notice how hard you've been practicing." Or, anything else to let her know how great she was doing. Tamaya often felt there were different rules for a captain. She was expected to do more. She wondered if anyone noticed how hard she was working?

Tamaya attempted her routine three more times. Each time was worse than the last. First it was the lack of flips. Then her foot slipped during her back-handspring landing.

And forget about the aerials. She couldn't even do one without her hands breaking her fall. Most days, Tamaya hated it when practice ended. Today she couldn't wait for the clock to strike six. When Coach Shelly said she'd see them tomorrow, Tamaya grabbed her bag, mumbled her goodbyes, and sped out of the gym.

"BUT I'M THE CAPTAIN!"

"Clear over the fence!" Tamaya's younger brother Jordan shouted, mouth full of roast potatoes. He waved his arms excitedly to show how far his teammate's ball was hit in the last game.

Pieces of potato fell out of Jordan's mouth and onto the table. They just missed Tamaya's plate. "That's so disgusting!" Tamaya said. She placed her arms around her plate to protect it.

"Sorry," Jordan said, grinning. He didn't look sorry. It didn't help that Tamaya's parents were trying not to laugh.

Tamaya moved her potatoes from one end of the plate to the other. She took a bite of her chicken and pushed it away. No one seemed to notice she was in a bad mood. She knew she was being childish, but she wanted to be noticed.

"I can't wait until next year," Jordan continued. "There are more games in seventh grade. That means more chances to be even better."

Tamaya made a production of covering her plate with her hands as another piece of potato flew out of Jordan's mouth. "Mom, can you please ask him to finish chewing before he talks? How am I supposed to eat this way?"

Tamaya's parents exchanged glances.

"Everything OK at school today?" asked Tamaya's dad.

Tamaya felt the tears again and swallowed. What was wrong with her? She was too old to be crying over gymnastics. She was too old to want so much attention.

"Practice didn't go well," she finally whispered.

"In what way?" asked Tamaya's mom.

"Our competition is in two weeks. I want a winning routine. I know my big combo could get me a great score. I just can't seem to put it all together." Tamaya stabbed a potato with her fork.

"Not the potato's fault," said Jordan.

Tamaya shot him a death glare. He rolled his eyes and went back to eating.

"You have time," said Tamaya's dad. "If you just keep practicing—"

"That's not enough!" Tamaya shouted. "Why does everyone keep saying that? I *am* practicing!"

"Tamaya," said her mom in a quiet but stern voice, "there's no need to yell."

"It's just . . . ," Tamaya began, but she wasn't sure what she wanted to say.

"Aren't you all a team?" asked Jordan. He made sure to finish chewing before speaking.

"Yeah. So what?" said Tamaya.

"Soo . . . ," he continued slowly, "it's not just about you. You all have routines to work on. The scores will balance each other out."

Tamaya scowled. "Gymnastics is not baseball. We have team scores. If my routine is awful, that won't help anyone."

"I get that," said Jordan, "but you always act like it's all about you—"

"I'm the captain!" Tamaya seethed.

Jordan raised his hands in surrender. "I know, I know. It's a lot of pressure."

"It is," said Tamaya quietly. "Coach Shelly told the other girls they were doing a good job. All she told me was to practice."

"I'm sure she knows how hard you're working," said Tamaya's mom gently.

"I guess," Tamaya muttered. "It wouldn't kill her to say that."

"You're captain," said Jordan. "She wouldn't have given you that title if she thought you stunk."

Tamaya opened her mouth to yell at her brother again, but her mom put her hand on her arm.

"Jordan, buddy," said Tamaya's dad, "how about you go start your homework? We'll call you when it's time for dessert."

"Gladly," said Jordan. "Things are getting too heated here."

When Jordan left, Tamaya's dad said, "Your brother is right, you know. Coach Shelly would not have made you captain lightly. She believes in you and knows how capable you are. Even if she doesn't always say it."

Tamaya shrugged. She just kept remembering Coach Shelly praise Fatima. She pictured her coach raving about Ivelisse's skills. Deep down, Tamaya knew Coach Shelly wouldn't have made her captain if she didn't believe in her. She still wanted her to say that out loud. She also knew that a good captain had to put aside her need to shine. Knowing that made Tamaya feel even worse.

CHAPTER 3

A CHANCE TO SHINE

Tamaya leaned forward in her seat as her gym teacher, Mr. Yochai, turned on the Smart Board. The class was studying famous athletes this week. Today's video was supposed to focus on the 2016 United States gymnastics team, known as the Final Five.

Yesterday's worries fled from her mind as Simone Biles and Aly Raisman appeared on the screen in front of her. These two gymnasts always inspired Tamaya.

Tamaya was blown away by both gymnasts' routines. She was amazed by Aly's efforts. Aly had missed medaling on the all-around in the 2012 Olympics. She didn't give up. She worked hard and came back in 2016 to win the silver.

Tamaya couldn't imagine putting in so much work only to have a medal slip away. She also didn't know if she'd have kept trying.

The video showed Aly's silver medal routine. Aly's routine included a double Arabian pass. Tamaya had not yet mastered that skill and imagined herself on the screen. She closed her eyes and went through the motions.

She pictured herself running down the mat. Her hands touched the mat as she launched herself into a round-off. Her legs snapped together in the air. She twisted her body to the side and brought her legs back down to the mat. She pushed off and completed two somersaults. She sailed high with her arms around her knees.

Like Aly, Tamaya landed perfectly. She didn't wobble in her imagination like she did in real life. Behind her closed lids, her hands didn't have to break her fall.

She heard the speakers in the class crackle. Suddenly Mr. Yochai was beside her.

"Better wake up," he said. "They want you in the office."

Tamaya's cheeks flushed red. "I wasn't sleeping. I was just—" She stopped midsentence. How would she explain? Saying she was imagining herself up there on the Smart Board was even more embarrassing than falling asleep in class. "Sorry. It won't happen again."

Tamaya grabbed her books and walked down to the office. Why did Ms. Davis want to see her?

She walked into the office and waited for someone to notice her. After a minute, she cleared her throat and spoke up. "Excuse me?" she began. "I was called down here?"

Her voice was scared and quiet, but she couldn't help it. What could she have possibly done wrong?

The secretary continued typing something on the computer and didn't look up. She just pointed to the open door of the principal's office. "Go on," she said when Tamaya stayed frozen on the stained gray carpet.

"Miss Jackson, come on in," called Principal Davis from inside her office.

Tamaya walked into her principal's office. She didn't know what she expected to see, but the flowered curtains and bright yellow couch surprised her. She didn't think a principal's office would look so cheery. She was also surprised to see Coach Shelly.

"Hi, Tamaya," said Coach Shelly warmly. "Have a seat."

The cheery room and her smiling coach made Tamaya less nervous. She sat beside Coach Shelly.

"We have some exciting news," said Principal Davis. She placed her palms on her desk. Her bright red hair matched perfectly with the room's colors.

"Our gymnastics program will be featured in a news broadcast!" said Coach Shelly.

Tamaya's heart beat quickly. "And I'll be on it?"

"Yes," said Coach Shelly, beaming. "That's why we asked you to come down. They will showcase the entire team. Since you're team captain, they'll spend more time with you."

"Really?" Tamaya jumped off the couch. She couldn't hold in her excitement. "I'll be on TV?"

Coach Shelly and Principal Davis exchanged looks. Tamaya wasn't sure why.

"You will be," said Principal Davis. "However, remember it's not about being a celebrity. As captain, you'll have to talk about the program."

Coach Shelly nodded. "You'll tell the reporters what you enjoy about the program and what you find challenging."

"And they'll see my routine?" Tamaya asked. That would mean she would have to work doubly hard to get it right.

Coach Shelly looked nervous. "They will, but I don't want you putting extra pressure on yourself."

"Right, right," said Tamaya, trying to look calm. It was impossible. She turned to Coach Shelly. "You'll help me with my routine then?"

Coach Shelly sighed. "Of course, but I'll have to work with the rest of the team too, and—"

"When are they coming?" Tamaya was getting anxious. Coach Shelly didn't seem to think helping Tamaya was important. The last thing Tamaya wanted was to look foolish in front of an audience.

"On Friday," said Coach Shelly.

"But that's only three days away!" Tamaya cried.

Coach Shelly put her hand on Tamaya's shoulder. "You'll be the spokesperson for the team.

Remember teamwork? It may make more sense if you saved your new routine for the competition and did something less challenging for the reporters. No reason to stress yourself out."

"Right," Tamaya said again. "Totally. Makes sense." Principal Davis and Coach Shelly smiled. Tamaya knew she'd said the right thing.

"Wonderful," said Principal Davis, clapping her hands. "Here are some forms for your parents to fill out saying they give you permission to participate."

"Thank you," said Tamaya. She tried to focus on what Coach Shelly was saying, but her mind had already left the room.

This would be her chance to show everyone what she was made of. She left the office and walked to her next class in a daze. She would be on TV just like Aly and Simone. She would finally get to shine!

CHAPTER 4

DISTRACTED

"Which angle would look best on camera?" asked Camiel. She touched the tips of her toes with her fingers for a deep stretch. She rolled onto her stomach and turned her head left then right.

Tamaya, Fatima, Ivelisse, and Natalia giggled and struck poses as well.

Coach Shelly shook her head and smiled. "The bigger question is how I should pose." She shook her head of shaggy, brown hair and placed a hand on her hip.

The gymnasts laughed and rolled their eyes.

"Seriously, though," said Coach Shelly, "don't let this special affect your focus. Our meet is in two weeks. We don't need any distractions."

Tamaya sprung up to turn a cartwheel. She followed it with a round-off and back handspring. "No distractions here," she said. Her voice wobbled, but she hoped no one noticed. She was very worried about making an error in front of the camera crew.

"Glad to hear it," said Coach Shelly. "I'd like to see everyone's routines. Ivelisse, start us off."

Ivelisse stood at the edge of the runway. She looked at the vault before her and nodded. She pumped her arms as she ran down the mat. *Bam!* Ivelisse's feet landed on the springboard, and she flew forward with power. Her hands reached for the vault as she pushed herself to handstand position.

Tamaya knew how much Ivelisse practiced and how on point each move had to be. She was always amazed at how easy Ivelisse made everything look.

Ivelisse pushed off from her handstand position on the vault. She zoomed down to the mat, like a torpedo. She landed in a perfect plie position, arms raised. Tamaya hoped her floor routine would be just as good.

"Natalia," called Coach Shelly, "come on down!"

Natalia jogged to the edge of the mat. She did a silly bow before beginning. Despite the hornets somersaulting in Tamaya's belly, she smiled at her teammate. She could always count on Natalia to lighten things up.

Like Ivelisse, Natalia pumped her arms as she sprinted down the runway. *Bam!* Her feet landed on the springboard. Her hands slammed on the vault. She launched into the air. Natalia's jump had an extra level of difficulty Ivelisse's did not. *Fwoop!* Natalia flipped in the air. *Wham!* Her feet thudded to the mat. She raised her arms in a perfect landing!

Tamaya wiped a bead of sweat from her forehead. Why was she so nervous?

Tamaya replayed her routine time and again in her mind. Each time, something else went wrong. It was like a bad movie she couldn't escape.

"Tamaya?" She felt a hand on her shoulder. "You OK?" whispered Camiel.

Tamaya nodded, but she felt hot. Her head spun. "I think I just need some water."

She grabbed her water bottle and took two big gulps. *Relax*, she told herself. *Don't think about the cameras.* She lifted her head and took another sip.

Once she went, she'd be fine. She knew it. "Coach? May I please go next?" she asked.

"Fine by me," said Coach Shelly. She motioned for the girls to follow her to the mat on the other side of the gym.

Tamaya got up slowly, legs shaking. She was never this nervous, not even before meets.

Warming up, she did a cartwheel, then a forward roll and a split jump where her legs rose in an upside-down V.

"Ready?" asked Coach Shelly.

Tamaya nodded and started her music. The floor routine was about looking both powerful and graceful. She pointed her left toe and raised her right arm over her head, like a C.

She heard the whir of the ceiling fan, but sweat still dripped down her face. She pumped her arms and bolted down the mat for her first tumbling pass. *Whoosh!* She flew into the air and tucked her knees to her chin. Two somersaults complete! She landed on the mat, pointed her toes, and curved her arms in front of her like she was holding an beach ball.

Graceful and powerful, she chanted in her head as she arched her back for her handspring. She did it! Time for two aerials. The fan sounded louder than before. *Whir. Whir. WHIR.*

Focus! Tamaya screamed the word in her head. She hoped it would help steady her nerves. It didn't work. She stood in the middle of the mat too scared to try the aerials.

"Let's take a break, girls," said Coach Shelly.

Tamaya didn't know what happened to her.

"It's just practice," said Ivelisse, squeezing her shoulder. "It happens to all of us."

Tamaya nodded, but she was worried. Jitters had never got the best of her before. If she psyched herself out at a normal practice, what would happen when the camera crews came? What would happen at the competition?

"Talk to me," said Coach Shelly. She sat cross-legged on the mat beside Tamaya.

Tamaya sat down beside her coach. "I don't know what's wrong with me. Aerials are tough, but I've done them before."

"I think you just have to gain confidence. Do basic moves you've mastered for a day or two. No pressure. That will help get your head back in the game," said Coach Shelly.

Tamaya knew her coach was right, but the camera crew was coming in two days.

"But the news special," she mumbled.

Coach Shelly sighed. "I was worried it would mess with your head. Do some handsprings. They look impressive on TV."

Tamaya could hear the annoyance in Coach Shelly's voice. Why didn't she understand how important this was for her?

Coach Shelly got up to work with the other girls. She heard her say, "Good job!" and, "Fine work!" and, "Way to go!" All Tamaya wanted was to hear the same.

She dragged her feet to the uneven bars to watch Fatima, but she couldn't focus. She closed her eyes and replayed her routine over and over. She wished she could complete picture-perfect aerials. No matter how hard she tried, the images behind her lids kept crashing to the mat.

CHAPTER 5

TV READY

Tamaya woke up the next morning feeling reenergized. She was ready for the reporters. *Blips happen to everyone,* she reminded herself. *No biggie.*

The day dragged. She sat in her classes and watched the minute hand slowly tick away. She wondered if the clocks were broken. No way could the school day be this long!

When the three o'clock bell rang, she was the first one out of her classroom. She ran to her locker, snatched her duffel bag, and flew to the gym locker room to change.

37

She had looked up which colors show up best on camera the night before. She chose her sparkly, red leotard.

Her teammates were already in the locker room when she got there.

"Did this day drag or what?" asked Camiel. She placed a bobby pin in her teeth as she pulled her highlighted hair into a ponytail. Tamaya noticed glitter in Camiel's hair. She must have researched on Google too.

"Not for me," chimed in Natalia, holding back a grin. "Is there something special today?"

Tamaya threw a rolled-up sock in her direction. Natalia ducked.

"I've been kind of worried about it," said Fatima. She chewed on her lip. "It's probably best if we listen to Coach Shelly. She said to pretend today is the same as any other day."

Tamaya laughed. If only she could do that! "I'm heading out," she said as she trotted to the gym.

The camera crew was already set up. Coach Shelly was speaking to a tall, blond woman in a burgundy suit.

"Tamaya!" Coach Shelly called. She waved to Tamaya to come over. "This is Mimi Pensallorto."

"Hi," said Tamaya shyly. She shook Mimi's hand. She looked tall from a distance, but was even taller up close. Tamaya's head reached just above Mimi's belly button.

"Your Coach tells me you're the captain of this team," said Mimi.

"I am." Tamaya noticed Mimi wasn't holding a mic. No cameras were focused on her either. She relaxed.

"I'm looking forward to learning more about this team and seeing everyone's routines," Mimi said. She leaned in and winked. "Especially yours."

"Me too," said Tamaya excitedly. This time, she wasn't nervous at all!

Mimi and the crew began filming at the beam. Tamaya sat on the bleachers with her teammates and watched as Camiel did a flawless routine.

Camiel jumped on the springboard, and hurled herself into the air. She did a somersault before landing on the beam. Tamaya had seen Camiel practice this mount many times. Often, her legs wobbled as she tried to gain balance on the four-inch-wide beam. Not today.

Camiel stood up confidently to continue, walking the beam with pointed toes. She jumped into the air. Her legs crisscrossed like scissors before touching the beam again.

Tamaya held her breath as Camiel got ready for her dismount. She ran down the beam, flew into the air, and did one flip before landing back on the mat. The camera crew applauded. Tamaya gave Camiel a thumbs-up.

Mimi twirled her finger in the air — a signal for the cameramen to move.

"Tamaya," she said, "can you show us some floor moves?"

"You got it!" said Tamaya. She hadn't felt this sure of herself in a long time. Adrenaline rushed through her body as she ran to the floor.

The second her music came on, Tamaya knew her routine would sing. She swayed her hips and pointed her toes. Her arms curved in pretty ballet poses. She thought of Simone and Aly as she completed her flips in the air. Her back arched for the perfect back handspring. At last it was time for the aerials.

Better to do just one, she thought. No need to risk falling. Tamaya kicked off into the air, her legs above her in a V. She landed on the mat. She had done it!

"That was impressive," said Mimi.

"Thank you," said Tamaya. She could barely believe she completed the routine without tripping or falling. "Aerials are hard for me."

"I wouldn't have guessed," said Mimi.

"That's why I practice all the time. Perfection isn't easy!" said Tamaya, winking.

Out of the corner of her eye, she saw Ivelisse shaking her head. *Do I sound too braggy?* Tamaya wondered. But there wasn't time to worry since Mimi fired one question after another.

Tamaya stared into the lights of the cameras and answered the best she could. Five minutes later, she couldn't even remember what she had said.

"Great job, ladies," said Coach Shelly after Mimi had left. "I can see how hard you all have been working."

Tamaya felt herself deflate. Why didn't Coach Shelly say she noticed *her* improvement? Just yesterday, she couldn't even complete her routine. Today, she did the aerial with no issues!

"The special will air over the weekend," said Coach Shelly. "Be prepared for fans!"

The girls laughed, and Tamaya knew she was joking. Even though the local paper had written about the special, Tamaya didn't think anyone would watch. Whenever they had meets, only parents showed up. But that didn't stop Tamaya from hoping Coach Shelly was right.

"You were awesome!" said Camiel as she and Tamaya walked to the locker room. "I even told the reporter what a great and supportive captain you are."

Tamaya gave Camiel a hug. "That's so sweet!"

Camiel looked around and lowered her voice. "I know Coach Shelly was kidding, but I hope we become a little famous. Is that bad?"

Tamaya grinned. She was so glad she wasn't the only one who felt that way! "Nope! Me too!"

The girls laughed. Tamaya imagined doing one aerial after another in front of the student body. They were all a team, but Tamaya was the captain. Shouldn't she count just a little bit more?

CHAPTER 6

FAMOUS

Tamaya and her teammates stretched out on the pillows surrounding Coach Shelly's TV. The living room table had bowls of cut-up veggies, pretzels, and whole-wheat mini pizzas.

"Thanks so much for having us over so we can watch the news special together!" said Camiel, mouth full of carrot. "This is so much better than fighting my little sister for the TV."

A piece of carrot fell out and landed on Tamaya's sock. "Ew, girl," she cried.

Camiel blushed. "Sorry," she said, placing her hand in front of her mouth.

"I'm just so glad my vault moves were on point," said Ivelisse.

"I'm just glad the whole thing is almost over," said Coach Shelly. "You all were getting a bit distracted. We have a meet next week."

Tamaya felt her coach's eyes rest on her. That seemed unfair. Everyone was getting distracted.

"*Shh, shh, shh!*" squealed Natalia, flapping her hands. "It's starting!"

Tamaya grabbed a handful of pretzels. She leaned back into the pillows as Mimi's long torso filled the screen. She spoke about the sport of gymnastics. She also showed clips of the 2012 United States Olympic Team — the Fierce Five — and the Final Five.

Tamaya stopped chewing as her idols graced the screen. Then Mimi showed clips of other schools and their teams.

Finally, images of Kennedy Middle School filled the TV. The red brick building looked more impressive on the screen than in real life. The big, gold letters spelling out Kennedy Middle School on the front of the building looked shinier than Tamaya remembered.

"Make it louder," said Fatima, searching for the remote.

"Did you know that Kennedy Middle School has the longest-running middle school gymnastics program in the state?" said Mimi. Her voice sounded more chipper than when Tamaya met her.

"It's you!" said Tamaya as Coach Shelly appeared on the special.

"The success of this team and program is all due to my gymnasts. They never shy away from a challenge and always support each other," said the TV Coach Shelly.

"That's so sweet. I think I'm going to cry," said Natalia.

"Shush," hissed Fatima. "They're showing the bars." The cameras zoomed in on Fatima releasing the higher bar, doing a flip in the air, and landing on the mat.

"Nice dismount," said Ivelisse.

"Yeah," said Fatima with a frown, "but I was hoping they were going to show the whole routine."

"They needed to film everyone, remember?" said Coach Shelly gently.

The screen flashed to Ivelisse and Natalia on the vault.

"What was that?" asked Natalia. "They showed Ivelisse running down the runway but finished with my landing! Like we're one person or something!"

"Our new name will be Ivelia!" said Ivelisse. She put her arm around Natalia. "It's cool we're even on it, right?" She smiled and crossed her eyes, and Natalia laughed.

"Oooh, it's you!" said Camiel as Tamaya flooded the screen.

Tamaya moved her pillow closer to the TV.

"And this team is led," began Mimi, "by their captain, eighth grader Tamaya Jackson."

Tamaya watched as the special played her whole routine, from start to finish. She shifted uncomfortably wondering how her teammates felt about that.

Tamaya listened to herself talk about how hard it was to do aerials and how much she practiced. She barely mentioned her teammates at all! How was that possible?

"And your team?" Mimi prompted.

TV Tamaya blinked. "Oh yeah," she said. She paused and stared into the camera. "They're great!"

Well, that was something at least, thought Tamaya. But why did she take so long to answer the question?

And why did Mimi have to remind her? Surely, she said more about them. The special just edited it out, right? She really couldn't remember.

The camera shot away from the gym, and Coach Shelly turned off the TV. No one said anything for a few seconds.

"That was cool, right?" said Ivelisse breaking the heavy silence. "I mean, Tamaya, how awesome that they showed your routine! Your aerial was perfect."

Tamaya was grateful that Ivelisse was being so nice.

"And they did talk about what a great program we have! Kudos to Coach Shelly for that!" said Natalia.

The mood was light again. Tamaya felt better by the time she went home. However, she was still struggling with her feelings. She was thrilled she was finally able to sparkle, but then she remembered Natalia's and Fatima's sad faces.

Jordan's words filled her thoughts, "Aren't you all a team?" She hoped this special wouldn't do anything to change that.

* * *

"What is happening?" asked Ivelisse as she elbowed her way into the gym.

Crowds of students were blocking the doorway. Others were seated around the edge of the gym.

"They're here to see Kennedy's newest celebrities," said Coach Shelly, shaking her head. "I was afraid this would happen."

Camiel clutched Tamaya's hand. "Oh my gosh! We were so hoping for this!" she squealed.

Tamaya nodded excitedly as Coach Shelly shot them both a death glare. "Our meet is next week. We can't afford distractions. Got it?" she said.

"Yes, ma'am!" all the girls said in unison. But Coach Shelly didn't smile.

While Tamaya's teammates went to practice on their apparatuses, Tamaya jogged to the mat for her floor routine. She warmed up with stretching, splits, cartwheels, and basic tumbling.

"Go, Tamaya!" someone shouted from the hallway.

Tamaya beamed and turned on her music.

She put extra energy into her routine, pushing off harder from the mat. She felt the power boosting her into the air for her somersault. Tamaya's toes graced the mat. She barely rested before launching into her back handspring.

Next it was aerial time! One, two! She had landed both hands-free cartwheels!

Nailed it! she thought. *Maybe I could do one more.*

She felt everyone watching her. Her breathing was shallow, but she ignored it. She kicked off with her back leg to launch herself into the air. Just like in practice days ago, her torso twisted too much.

Tamaya felt herself falling to the ground. She landed on her arm with a thud. Pain shot to her shoulder, and she screamed.

"Tamaya!" Ivelisse shouted running to her. She offered Tamaya her hand to help her up.

Please let nothing be broken. Please, Tamaya pleaded. She carefully sat up and moved her arm around. She slowly moved it in circles. It hurt a little, but nothing some ice wouldn't help. "I'm fine," she said.

Ivelisse ran to get ice. When she returned, she sat beside Tamaya on the mat. "How did that happen?"

"What do you mean? I fell. Everyone makes mistakes." There was an edge to Tamaya's voice. She wished she could take it back. Ivelisse was only being nice.

"Was it on the aerial?" Ivelisse asked.

Tamaya nodded. "I tried to do three in a row and—"

"Why?" Ivelisse's voice rose. She looked around the gym. Kids had their phones out recording their practice. "Oh, I get it." She looked disappointed.

Tamaya sprang to her feet. Ivelisse's knowing tone and frown annoyed her. "Like you don't want them all to see how good you are!" she said a little too loudly.

Ivelisse closed her eyes then opened them again. Tamaya knew this was something her friend did when she was trying to calm down. "Sure, I do," Ivelisse said, "but perfecting my routine for next week's meet is first. Our *team* comes first."

Ivelisse just doesn't get it, thought Tamaya. The gym was crowded with students, but no one was calling out Ivelisse's name. Tamaya almost said that but stopped herself. That would just have been too mean.

"I'm going to go home," said Tamaya.

"You do that," said Ivelisse, walking away. "And while you're icing, think about what it means to be part of a team."

"I do think about the team!" Tamaya called after her. Her words got lost in the noise of the gym. Or, maybe, she never said them that loudly at all.

CHAPTER 7

FALLING OUT

Tamaya hoped the crowds would thin. Three days later the gym was still packed. Her teammates somehow blocked out the noise better than she could. It didn't help that there was always a bigger crowd around Tamaya.

Tamaya still hadn't apologized to Ivelisse. She told herself Ivelisse wasn't ready to accept the apology anyway. *I'll just try talking with her and see what happens,* thought Tamaya. She chose a spot beside Ivelisse for stretching.

"Can you believe we're the thing to watch around here?" asked Tamaya. She pulled her left knee to her chest.

Ivelisse placed her legs into straddle position. She lowered her elbows to the mat. "I guess there's nothing good on YouTube," she said.

Tamaya reached for her right elbow. She pulled it toward her left shoulder. She had iced her shoulder the day she fell on it. It still hurt a little. She winced.

Ivelisse noticed the look of pain on Tamaya's face. "Don't let the fans distract you today."

Tamaya glared at her. Ivelisse's words about Tamaya putting herself above the team still stung. She learned her lesson about trying to do too much. Why did Ivelisse have to harp on that again?

"Wasn't planning on it," she said. She moved to a spot away from Ivelisse. Ivelisse sighed, but Tamaya ignored it.

Kids raised their phones to record her moves. Tamaya felt the familiar hornets in her stomach. Her fall from last practice was all over the Internet. Couldn't people just watch without recording?

Shake it off, she told herself.

She rolled her neck. She pretended her arms were strings of spaghetti. She waved them around to ease her jitters. Tamaya did easy moves to get her confidence back. A cartwheel, then a round off, a split, a simple back handspring, and forward roll.

She was getting calmer with each move. She'd be thrilled if only these moves were posted online. She'd be even happier if all phones just disappeared. *You got this,* Tamaya told herself.

She turned on her music. She focused on the familiar notes. She curved her arm and pointed her toes. She did a small hop and launched herself into her sequence. She felt light as she soared through the air for her flip.

Her toes touched the ground with a soft thunk. She heard voices around her but tried to block them out. *Focus.*

Her arms reached behind her. Tamaya arched her back. Her feet flew over her head as she completed her back handsprings. Only the aerials were left. This time, she'd only do one. She didn't want to hurt her shoulder more. She didn't need to be a hero.

She kicked off with her back leg. She clenched her fists. She didn't want to accidentally touch the ground. Tamaya twisted her body to the right. *Boom!* She landed. Her legs stumbled. She touched the ground to regain her balance. But she didn't fall!

Her shoulder was a little stiff but not too bad. She had done it! She looked around her. Her pride quickly vanished.

Kids whispered and snickered. "Nice job not falling!" someone called out.

There was no point in yelling back. So what that she stumbled. She didn't fall. Did they all think this was easy?

Tears pushed at the corners of Tamaya's eyes. She turned away, but there was nowhere to go. Everyone was watching. The competition was next week. She had to practice. But how?

She couldn't concentrate here. She couldn't do her routine without worrying about every mistake showing up online. She could only imagine how Olympic gymnasts felt. So many more people judged and taped them!

Tamaya walked over to the bars to watch Fatima. She was in the zone. Her face was serious. Tamaya could tell Fatima only had the bars on her mind. How did she do it?

Fatima began with the kip mount. She jumped from the floor and grabbed the lower bar. Her legs snapped together as she reached her pointed toes to the bar.

Tamaya could see Fatima's stomach muscles tighten as she leaned forward. She lifted her hips so they rested on the bar. She completed a flip and pushed herself into a handstand on the lower bar. Her body was straight, like a candlestick.

Tamaya knew what came next. She watched as Fatima came out of her handstand and reached for the high bar. Tamaya had seen her miss the grip before. She didn't miss it today. The crowd clapped. Tamaya felt a twinge of jealousy but shook it off. Fatima deserved all that praise. Her routine was almost over. The hardest parts were still to come.

Fatima caught her breath before launching into the giant. She rose into a handstand on the high bar. She swung her legs down. She rose back up into a handstand. Her legs and body traveled around the bar three times. Fatima gained more power each time. Finally, she released the high bar. She did one flip in the air and landed on the mat.

Tamaya knew Fatima wouldn't stick the landing the second she saw the position of her left foot. It was too far from the right. After her feet hit the mat, Fatima fell on her bottom.

There went the phones again. Tamaya heard snickers. She bit her lip, feeling sorry for her friend. She looked at Fatima. She was fine! She stood up, shrugged, and started from the beginning.

Tamaya was amazed. How was Fatima able to ignore everyone around her?

She looked at her other teammates. They were practicing as usual. They weren't letting their mistakes bother them.

What is wrong with me? Tamaya wondered. Why couldn't she ignore the craziness around her too?

CHAPTER 8

MAKING UP

That night, Tamaya picked at her spaghetti. Jordan was talking about some kid who sprayed milk through his nose at lunch. Their dad talked about something funny that happened at work.

Tamaya was barely paying attention. She only knew it was funny because Jordan and her mom kept laughing. Everyone looked at her. They must have asked her a question, but Tamaya didn't know what it was. She kept replaying the last few days over and over in her head.

"Hello?" said Jordan, waving his hand in front of Tamaya's face. "Earth to Tamaya. Any living things on your planet?"

Tamaya swatted his hand away and narrowed her eyes. "There will be one *less* living thing if you don't leave me alone."

"Here we go again," Jordan mumbled. "Must be another bad day at practice."

"Is that the reason for the long face?" asked Tamaya's dad.

Tamaya stared at her plate. She twirled the spaghetti pieces on her fork. She was afraid she'd cry if she tried to speak. She didn't want to give Jordan more reasons to make fun of her.

"Jordan," said Tamaya's mom, "can you give us a few minutes to talk to Tamaya alone?"

Jordan put his plate in the sink and grabbed a brownie. "It's a far walk from here to the family room," he said with a grin. "I need the extra energy."

"Ever since that special aired," began Tamaya's dad, "you haven't been yourself."

Tamaya couldn't stop the tears. She was glad her brother wasn't in the room. "I thought the attention would be exciting. It's just making me nervous."

"Why?" asked Tamaya's mom. She stroked Tamaya's hair. "Didn't you say everyone saw you on TV?"

Tamaya nodded. "That's just it. The gym is always packed with people. They're always recording. Every time I make a mistake, everyone sees it."

"How do the other girls feel about this? What about your coach?" asked Tamaya's dad.

Tamaya dabbed at her eyes with her napkin. "The other girls all seem fine. I haven't really talked to my coach. Or the team."

"Why's that?" asked Tamaya's mom gently.

Tamaya sniffed and shrugged.

"Oh hon," said Tamaya's mom. She pulled her in for a hug. "Why don't you start by doing just that?"

Tamaya reached for a clean napkin. She ran it through her fingers then shredded it.

"What would I even say to them?" she asked.

Tamaya's mom cocked her head to the side. "It will come to you."

Tamaya picked up a piece of napkin and shredded it some more. Her mom made it sound easy. The truth was things have been so weird between her and her friends.

Tamaya buried her face in her mom's shirt. She felt like a little kid but didn't mind. "I guess," she said. But she knew making the first move with her team wouldn't be easy.

* * *

Tamaya was the first to get to the gym Saturday morning. She was thankful it was the weekend. Only school club and sports teams were allowed.

That meant there would be no one watching. Her every mistake wouldn't be posted online.

Tamaya warmed up with stretching. She also practiced on the other equipment. She stood at the end of the runway to the vault and pumped her arms as she ran. She jumped over the vault with ease. She didn't stumble on her landing.

The balance beam was next. She decided to challenge herself with a front tuck mount onto the beam. Tamaya raised her hand in the air before beginning, just like she would do at the Orton meet. She ran down the mat and jumped onto the springboard. She somersaulted in the air and landed on the beam.

She was so proud of herself. She couldn't remember the last time she'd felt so proud. The last few days had been about what she *couldn't* do. Tamaya was feeling confident again. And happy. She knew she would be able to do her floor moves with no issues.

She walked away from the beam to start her floor routine. She turned on her music and began. Her hips swayed. Her arms curved. She bounced from one point of the mat to the other. Each move gave her more speed and power. She completed her back handsprings and took a quick breath.

Aerial time. Her left leg kicked up just as she'd planned. Her body was upside down and her legs in cartwheel mode. *Bam!* Her feet landed on the mat. No wobbling. No falling. She completed her second aerial with ease and finished with a split. Tamaya threw her hands in the air in triumph. "Yes!" she called to the empty gym.

Tamaya got up, still breathing hard. She finally did the kind of routine she'd been picturing in her head. To her surprise, that was enough. She didn't wish dozens of phones had captured her success.

"Nice!" she heard from the gym's entrance.

Tamaya spun around and saw her team there. She tried to read the expressions on their faces.

Were they annoyed with her? Was Ivelisse still mad at her? There was only one way to find out.

Tamaya slowly walked over to her team. Her feet felt like they were dragging through mud. She hoped her mother was right about the words coming to her.

"Hey," said Tamaya when she approached her teammates. It wasn't much, but it was a start. She looked down at her feet.

Someone cleared her throat. Someone else coughed.

"All your hard work paid off," said Coach Shelly. "That was a fantastic routine."

Tamaya raised her head. "Really?"

Coach Shelly smiled warmly. "Of course," she said, putting her arm around Tamaya's shoulders. "I hope you're as proud of yourself as I am."

Tamaya didn't think she could grin any wider. She felt like puppet strings were pulling at the corners of her mouth.

"I didn't think you noticed how hard I'd been working," she said softly.

Coach Shelly looked surprised. "Then I apologize. I knew your combinations were tough, but I had faith you'd get them. I should have realized you needed some attention too."

Tamaya looked at her feet again. "I'm sorry about how I acted." Her face reddened. "I just wanted to be noticed."

Natalia gently nudged Tamaya's shoulder with her own. "We *all* want attention sometimes," she said. "I was jealous the special focused on you."

"Me too," the other girls said.

Tamaya raised her head, feeling better. Her cheeks still felt a little hot. "I'm glad I'm not the only one who felt left out. But I *am* the only one who got so distracted."

"No more fans," said Coach Shelly. "I told Principal Davis we need to focus."

The girls cheered.

"I was *not* thrilled they captured my every mistake," said Fatima.

Coach Shelly beamed at her team. "I think we all learned a lot from this experience. Tamaya, I'll begin today's practice with you." She winked at her.

"Thank you, Coach," said Tamaya.

As the girls left to stretch, Tamaya tapped Ivelisse on the shoulder. She took a deep breath. "I wanted to apologize the most to you," she said. "You've been so nice, and I kept snapping at you. You were right. I didn't put the team first."

Ivelisse put her arm around Tamaya. "Don't worry about it. We all have our ups and downs. I know you care about us and the team."

"I really do," said Tamaya.

"And I want you to know," said Ivelisse, "what a great captain you've been. You always motivate me to do better."

Tamaya's smile sparkled. This time, Ivelisse's words were all she needed to shine.

CHAPTER 9

MAKING THE BAR

The purple sequins on Tamaya's leotard twinkled as she walked into the brightly lit gym at Orton High School. It was three times bigger than the gym at Kennedy. The walls were painted a sunny yellow. The equipment looked new and shiny. The stands were full.

The excitement in the room made Tamaya's heart soar. Today she didn't mind the crowds. Most of all, she loved that her family was in the bleachers.

"Isn't this place wild?" asked Natalia.

"Totally," said Ivelisse. "It looks like it ate our gym for dinner and dessert."

Fatima and Camiel cracked jokes too. But Tamaya stayed silent and took it all in. She thought about how hard she and her teammates worked the last few weeks and how far she'd come. She was surprised she didn't feel jittery. She only felt calm.

"You girls ready?" asked Coach Shelly. "I know you'll knock it out of the park."

The girls piled their hands one on top of the other and yelled, "Go Kennedy!"

"I want you to know how proud I am of all of you," said Coach Shelly. "Whatever happens today, I will know you tried your best."

The speakers in the gym crackled as a voice announced a ten-minute warning. As Tamaya and her teammates stretched, she looked around the gym at the other competitors.

Orton, in their green, rhinestone-studded leotards, was on the opposite side of the gym. Their faces looked fierce and focused.

Tamaya also recognized the orange leotards from Jefferson, a nearby town. These gymnasts looked more relaxed. They sat near the bleachers, smiling and cracking jokes.

But every few minutes, Tamaya saw one of them glance at her and the Orton team and bite her lip. *Maybe they aren't so relaxed after all*, thought Tamaya.

The Summit gymnasts, dressed in soft-looking blue leotards, stretched near Orton. Tamaya heard good things about all three teams. She didn't know which one Kennedy should worry about the most.

Plus, there were teams scattered throughout the gym in a rainbow of leotards and sparkles. Tamaya didn't recognize many of them. Maybe *those* were the teams to beat.

"I feel like I'm going to throw up," whispered Fatima as she studied the other teams. She wiped her sweaty palms on her knees.

Tamaya felt her nerves creep up too. She pushed them away and put her arm around her friend. "You'll be great," she said. "You're always so confident on the bars."

Fatima laughed. "I fake it well."

The buzzer rang. Fatima gave Tamaya a worried look.

"Just think. In a few minutes it will be over," said Tamaya with a smile.

"One way or another," Fatima mumbled. She jogged to the bars.

Tamaya watched her teammate from the bench. Just like in practice, Fatima began with the kip. She seemed to hold herself up longer today. That was a good start. She did a handstand on the lower bar. *Fwoosh!* Her legs sailed down, and she reached for the high bar.

Tamaya saw the look of determination on Fatima's face. The giant was next. Fatima rose into a handstand on the high bar. Her body circled the bar one, two, three times.

There was only the dismount left. Tamaya remember how Fatima stumbled during practice. There were more people here today. She hoped Fatima could block them out.

Fatima swung around the bar one more time. She released and flipped twice. Her feet hit the mat. She straightened her body. Her hands shot up into the air. The crowd cheered, and Fatima beamed and waved. It was a perfect landing!

"Wonderful!" yelled Coach Shelly over the noise in the gym as the team gathered around Fatima.

"That was killer!" said Camiel.

"See?" said Tamaya. "I knew you could do it."

"And you will too," said Fatima.

Tamaya hoped she was right.

* * *

Tamaya chewed her nail and watched an
Orton gymnast take the floor. The girl's red hair
was tied with a green ribbon to match her leotard.

She raised her hand in the air and jutted out
her hip. As soon as her rock medley began, the
gymnast sprang into action. Tamaya's throat went
dry as she watched the Orton girl nail every flip.
Her feet rebounded off the mat quickly. She didn't
pause between moves. Tamaya was certain the girl
caught her breath, but she couldn't tell when.

The music sped up, and the gymnast's red
ponytail bobbed as she ran down the mat. *Phwt!*
Phwt! She completed two flips in the air before
landing on her feet. The crowd applauded, and
Tamaya swallowed nervously.

The gymnast's hair was a trail of fire behind
her as she cartwheeled down the mat for her grand
finale. Tamaya leaned forward in her bleacher seat.

She held her breath as she recognized the girl's stance. She was going to do an aerial!

She launched herself in the air. Her hands stayed at her sides and her legs flew in the air. Perfect landing!

Tamaya closed her eyes and tried to calm her racing heart as she quickly compared her routine to Orton's. She had two aerials, and the Orton gymnast only had one. But the second wouldn't help her if she didn't complete it. Orton's routine was flawless. Tamaya's better be too.

* * *

There were two more groups before Tamaya's turn on the floor. She watched as Jefferson's orange leotards flew high in the air off the vault. They reminded Tamaya of blazing suns.

Her glance shifted to a Summit gymnast on the beam. The gems on the blue leotard shimmered under the ceiling lights.

She somersaulted on the beam and stuck the landing. Her body didn't lean. The flawlessness of the other teams made Tamaya feel hot. She turned away and focused on her teammates.

"Go Ivelisse!" she cheered loudly. Anything to stop her brain from replaying "what ifs."

Ivelisse stood at the end of the runway. She raised one hand high in the air. This signaled to the judges that she was ready.

Tamaya flashed back to the news special that blended Natalia and Ivelisse into one. Today they both had the chance to show their great routines.

Ivelisse pumped her arms. She gained speed as she ran down the runway. Her feet slammed onto the springboard. Her hands hit the vault. She flew into the air like an upside-down rocket.

Tamaya knew the landing wasn't easy because Ivelisse could not see the mat from her angle. She held her breath. She wondered if the audience was doing the same.

Stomp! Ivelisse's feet planted on the mat. She threw her arms up and grinned. Tamaya giggled at the happy and surprised look on Ivelisse's face.

"You did it, girl!" Tamaya cheered.

Ivelisse was out of breath. All she could do was smile and nod in Tamaya's direction.

CHAPTER 10

TEAMWORK

Before Tamaya's turn on the floor, it was Camiel's turn on the beam.

Camiel bounced off the springboard and mounted the beam with a somersault. Like in practice, Camiel's landing was tight. Her feet did not get too close to the beam's edge. She walked along the beam with pointed toes.

Tamaya leaned forward as Camiel readied herself for a new move, a backward flip. She arched her back and raised her hands in the air.

Her right foot kicked high into the air. Her left foot followed closely.

Camiel's legs sliced like scissors in the air before successfully landing on the beam. Camiel lowered her chest and raised her left leg behind her. She held the balance pose like a flamingo.

Only a split leap left and a dismount, thought Tamaya. *You can do it.*

Camiel jumped. Her legs performed a split in midair before landing back on the beam. She ran down the beam. She catapulted off the end of the beam and flipped. She landed on the mat perfectly. She thrust her arms in the air and grinned.

Tamaya mentally scored Camiel's routine and hoped the difficulty level was enough for Camiel to take the beam. The buzzer brought Tamaya out of her thoughts. It was finally her turn.

She tried to calm the voices in her head. She knew her routine. She'd practiced. She closed her eyes and took a deep breath.

Tamaya walked over to the mat. She made eye contact with the judges and nodded. Her music flowed and erased her worries. Tamaya felt light as her toes pointed. She sashayed down the mat. She dropped to the floor, rolled onto her stomach, and grabbed her ankles. She pulled her head toward them and arched her back.

Then Tamaya was back on her feet. The music sped up. She bounced off the balls of her feet and somersaulted in the air twice. *Boom!*

Her toes touched the mat. She leaned back and threw her arms behind her. Her legs leaped off the floor and over her head. The crowd roared at Tamaya's perfect back handspring. She kept her focus.

Two aerials to go, she thought. She was in the moment, just like the title of her song.

Tamaya raised her left leg forward while hopping on her right. She planted her left leg on the mat and lowered her arms to her waist.

She kicked with her back leg and flew into the air. Her legs made a V above her head. Her arms tucked at her sides. *Bam!* She landed on the mat.

One more time! Tamaya repeated the moves. *Thwack!* Her feet planted easily. She sank into a split and raised her arms. She had done two aerials to Orton's one. And they were perfect.

Tamaya waved her hands in the air and caught her breath. She had done her best and didn't psych herself out. She'd find out soon if that was enough.

* * *

Tamaya, Fatima, Camiel, Natalia, and Ivelisse stood on the podium. They linked their arms and held them high. Gold medals hung around their necks. Cameras snapped photos, and phones recorded. When the girls stepped off the podium, reporters shoved microphones in their faces.

"I was excited to see the special about your team," said a dark-haired male reporter.

He aimed his phone at Tamaya. "What does winning another competition mean?"

"It shows how strong our team and coach are," said Tamaya.

"How do you, as team captain, help your team succeed?" the reporter continued.

Tamaya paused. A couple weeks ago, she would have jumped at an opportunity like this. She would have wanted to talk about how hard her routine was. She would have loved the attention. But today she looked at her teammates who were also answering questions.

"It's not just me," said Tamaya, grinning. "We all work hard and motivate each other. We need one another to be our best." She motioned for her teammates to come over and speak to the reporter.

The sun streamed through the windows. It shone brightly on her team's gold medals and sequined leotards. Tamaya beamed. She shined brightest with her teammates around her.

ABOUT the AUTHOR

Margaret Gurevich is the author of many books for kids, including Capstone's *Chloe by Design* series and *Gina's Balance*, a *Sports Illustrated Kids* story from the *What's Your Dream?* series. She has also written for *National Geographic Kids* and Penguin Young Readers. This is her third book about gymnastics, but her characters are much better gymnasts than she ever was. When she's not writing, she likes exercising, spending time with her family and friends, reading, and watching movies.

GLOSSARY

adrenaline (uh-DREN-uh-lin)—a chemical produced by your body when you are excited, frightened, or angry

apparatus (ap-uh-RAT-uhss)—equipment used for performing gymnastics

dismount (diss-MOUNT)—a move by which a gymnast gets off an apparatus or finishes a floor exercise, usually landing upright on the feet

momentum (moh-MEN-tuhm)—the force or speed that a person or an object has while moving

routine (roo-TEEN)—a combination of skill elements on one apparatus or event

sequence (SEE-kwuhnss)—two or more skills which are performed together, creating a different combination skill

springboard (SPRING-bord)—a flexible board used in gymnastics to help a person jump high in the air

tumbling pass (TUHM-buhl-ing PASS)—a series of connected tumbling skills during a floor exercise

uneven bars (uhn-EE-vuhn BARS)—an apparatus featuring two parallel bars placed at different heights and widths, allowing the gymnast to transition from bar to bar

DISCUSSION QUESTIONS

1. There are several conflicts in Tamaya's story. Discuss them in your own words. Which is the main conflict?

2. How does the title *Aerials and Envy* relate to the story? Can you think of other titles that would also work?

3. What characteristics are important in a team captain? Does Tamaya have those characteristics?

WRITING PROMPTS

1. We follow Tamaya in this story. Imagine you are one of the other gymnasts, and write a journal entry of how you felt after seeing the news special.

2. Do you think that Ivelisse would be a good team captain? Write a paragraph to explain your answer, using examples from the book.

3. Write a newspaper article covering the gymnastics meet. Be sure to include quotes from the star gymnasts.

MORE ABOUT
GYMNASTICS

The Fierce Five was made up of gymnasts Jordyn Wieber, Gabby Douglas, Aly Raisman, McKayla Maroney and Kyla Ross. And the team was fierce: They won a gold medal for the United States! Gabby Douglas also won an all-around gold medal, and McKayla Maroney won silver for the vault. Aly Raisman took home a gold medal for floor and bronze for the balance beam!

Did you know, though, that they were first called the Fab Five? Turned out that name was already taken by University of Michigan's 1991 men's basketball team. The girls needed a new name. McKayla Maroney and Jordyn Wieber decided they would come up with a creative one. They searched on their phones for words that started with the letter F that could describe their team. The finalists were *fierce* and *feisty*. McKayla said she liked *fierce* the best because ". . . we are definitely the fiercest team out there."

In 2016, the United States won team gold again! The Final Five was made up of Aly Raisman, Gabby Douglas, Simone Biles, Madison Kocian, and Laurie Hernandez. Simone won a team gold, individual all-around gold, and gold medals in the floor exercise and vault. She also won a bronze on the balance beam. In addition to the team gold, Aly won a silver on floor. This made up for her losing the tie breaker and bronze medal in the all-around in the 2012 Olympics.

The 2016 team name has a great story behind it too! The girls chose "Final Five" as a tribute to Coach Martha Karoyli who retired after the 2016 Olympics. They were the last, or final, team she coached. The name also has another meaning. 2016 was also the last Olympics with five gymnasts on a team. All U.S. Olympic teams will now have only four members.